Panther in the Sky by Brigitte Brown Jackson



ISBN 978-0-578-52814-4

Printed in the United States of America.

Ubuntu Press © 2019
PO Box 524
Flint, MI 48501
www.ubuntupress.org

To my uncle, Mark Clark, who sacrificed so that others may have a more fulfilled life.

To my loving husband for all of his support, my children who inspired me to transform my dreams, and my parents for always believing in me.

In loving memory of Kimberly Outlaw Springer and Vickie Patterson for the support and encouragement in the writing of this book many years ago.

Ebony was so excited. It was her first day of school. She had been looking forward to this day all summer.

Ebony eagerly grabbed her mother's hand as they stepped off the porch. She said, "Mom, tell me Uncle's story again."

Ebony's mom replied, "Sure, but let's get you in your seatbelt first."   Ebony's mom snapped the seatbelt in place.

Then, in her Big Momma story-telling voice, she began telling the story of Uncle.

“The panther in the sky could be seen all the way down MacArthur Highway. I knew I was getting close to the building. I was always excited when I saw the yellow eyes of the black panther. Soon I would be helping pass out the breakfast to the children. I loved giving out the food with Uncle. The smell of food would fill the entire room.”

“More,” Ebony bellowed.

“Alright, I’m telling the story,” mom quickly exclaimed.

“I would help Uncle give out the hot breakfast to all the neighborhood children before they started their walk to school. He knew if children were hungry, they could not learn in school. Uncle and the Black Panther Party worked hard to teach the children in the neighborhood about how important it was to know black history. They taught things they didn’t teach at school. They also taught them how to read and do math. Uncle was so smart. I loved when he walked me to the headquarters. I knew it would be an exciting day.”

Ebony cut mom off, “Mommy, get to the good part.”

Mom finished telling the story. “Uncle picked me up and gently sat me on the counter. He told me about how strong, intelligent and beautiful we are as black people.

His face beamed with pride as he raised his fist in the black power salute, saying,

***All Power to the People***.”

"He told me that he and the Black Panther Party had a war on poverty.  Uncle always explained the big words to me.

He knew I **LOVED** big words."

"I liked to use them to impress people. He would explain that a war is when you fight against someone who is against you. Then he'd go on and tell me that poverty was when you don't have the things you need to survive. That's why we fed the children a hot breakfast before going to school, he would often say with a serious look in his eyes."

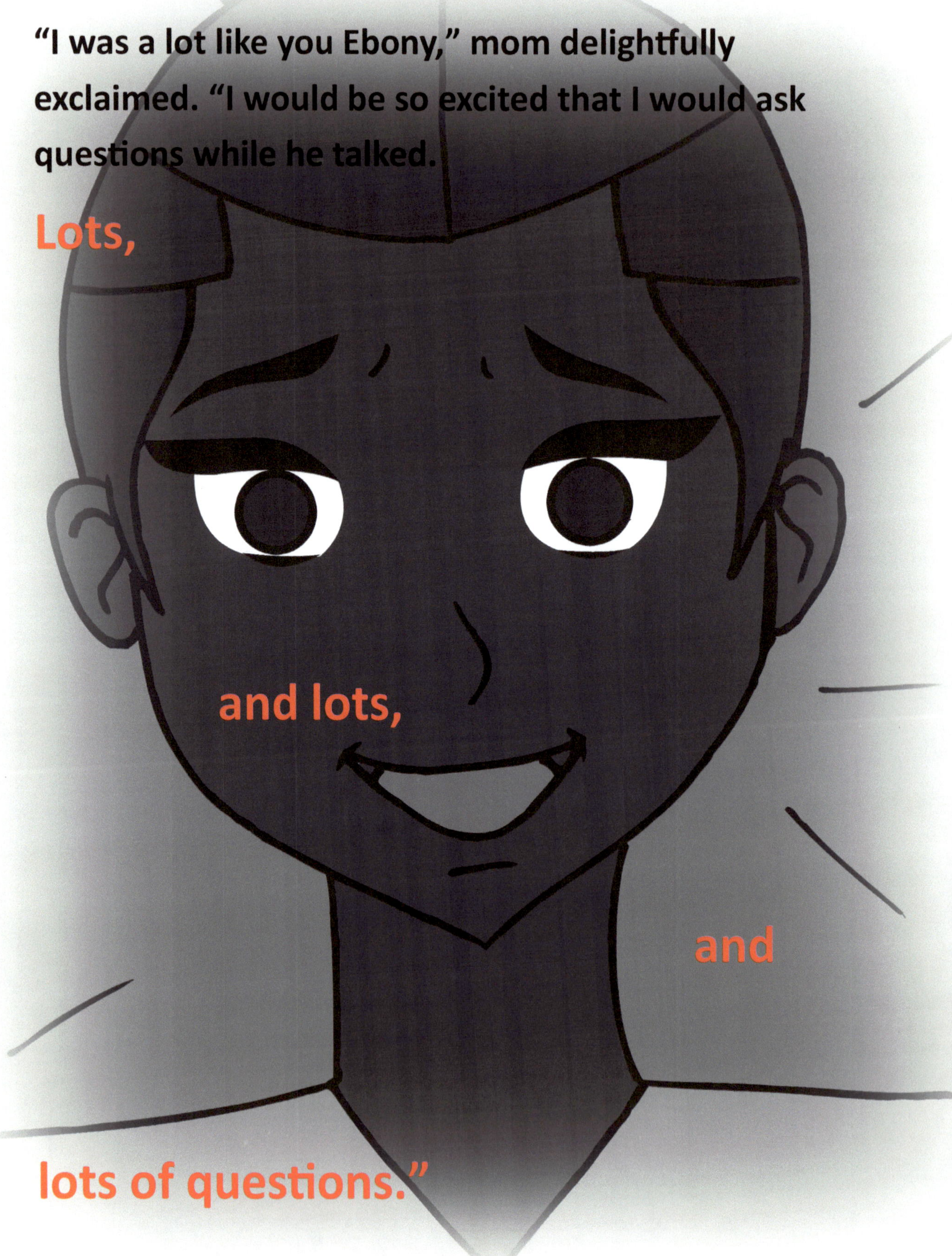

**"I was a lot like you Ebony," mom delightfully exclaimed. "I would be so excited that I would ask questions while he talked.**

**Lots,**

**and lots,**

**and**

**lots of questions."**

"He was my hero.
He was always generous to me. Uncle loved children."

"Uncle was an amazing leader. He was a civil rights activist. That meant he loved helping people in the community and making it a better place to live, work, play, and buy goods and services. He was learning from other activists in other cities. The Black Panthers passed out free food and clothes across the country. They helped the elderly and they helped the community get medical care."

"Free clothes? Why?" Ebony questioned.

"Ebony, we are almost at school so let me finish the story," mom whispered to her. Peeking in the rear view mirror, she continued. "They gave out free clothes because everyone wasn't as blessed as you. They couldn't afford to go to the store and buy new clothes. Many of the people lived in poverty."

Ebony chimed in,

**"Okayyyyyyyyy!**

**Okayyyyyyyyy!**

I remember you said poverty is when you don't have enough money to survive."

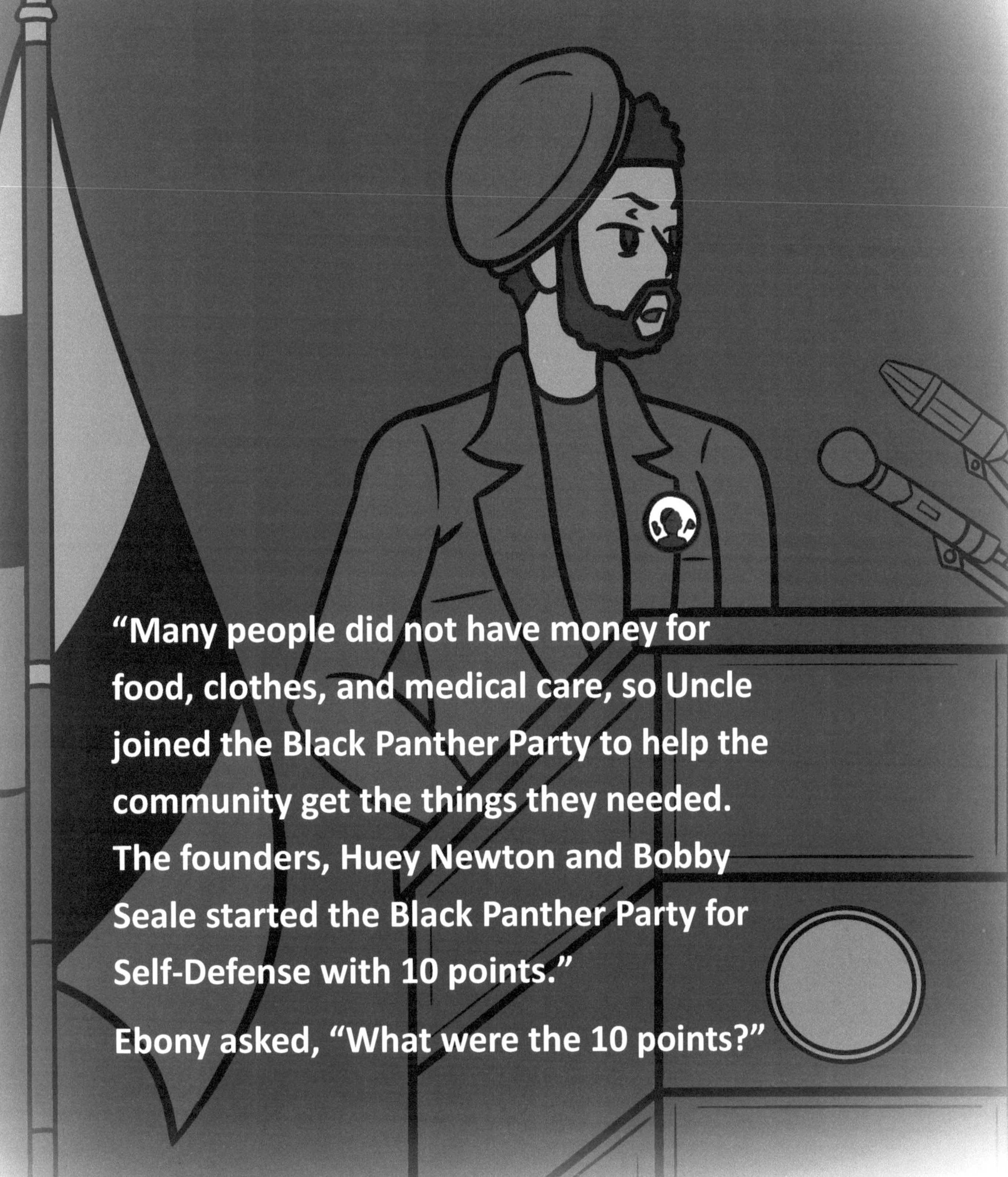

"Many people did not have money for food, clothes, and medical care, so Uncle joined the Black Panther Party to help the community get the things they needed. The founders, Huey Newton and Bobby Seale started the Black Panther Party for Self-Defense with 10 points."

Ebony asked, "What were the 10 points?"

Mom answered, "Well, they had 10 rules to tell others what they wanted for the community. It's like your dad and I teaching you about civics. The 10 points are like your social contract at school. The Black Panthers wanted the government or people that make laws, or rules, to agree to do these ten things. It was an agreement of behaviors. "

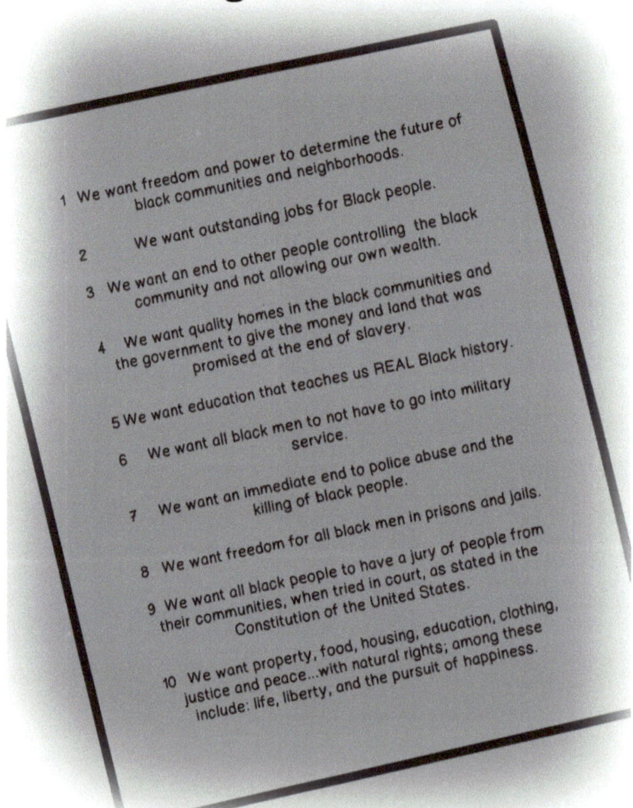

1 We want freedom and power to determine the future of black communities and neighborhoods.

2 We want outstanding jobs for Black people.

3 We want an end to other people controlling the black community and not allowing our own wealth.

4 We want quality homes in the black communities and the government to give the money and land that was promised at the end of slavery.

5 We want education that teaches us REAL Black history.

6 We want all black men to not have to go into military service.

7 We want an immediate end to police abuse and the killing of black people.

8 We want freedom for all black men in prisons and jails.

9 We want all black people to have a jury of people from their communities, when tried in court, as stated in the Constitution of the United States.

10 We want property, food, housing, education, clothing, justice and peace...with natural rights; among these include: life, liberty, and the pursuit of happiness.

In unison, Ebony and mom said,

"Ubuntu means, I am because you are."

"Uncle used the 10 rules and started working in our community. He wanted everyone in Peoria to have a better life. And he worked very hard. Uncle loved working."

“One Fall day, Uncle walked hand-in-hand with me, but he was different. I could tell. He was quiet. So, I asked him what was wrong. He told me he was leaving our city and going to another city to do some bigger work. It made me so sad to hear this because I loved to walk with Uncle each morning and listen to him talk about things he read in books.”

“Uncle was an amazing civil rights activist. He loved serving people in his neighborhood.”

“That was my last walk with Uncle. He left to make a change. He believed he could help people and he did! But soon after, Uncle was killed by some mean people that did not want him to help his people get out of poverty and have a better life.”

“So, he was killed like Martin Luther King Jr., Malcolm X, and Medgar Evers?” Ebony asked.

“Yes,” mom replied.

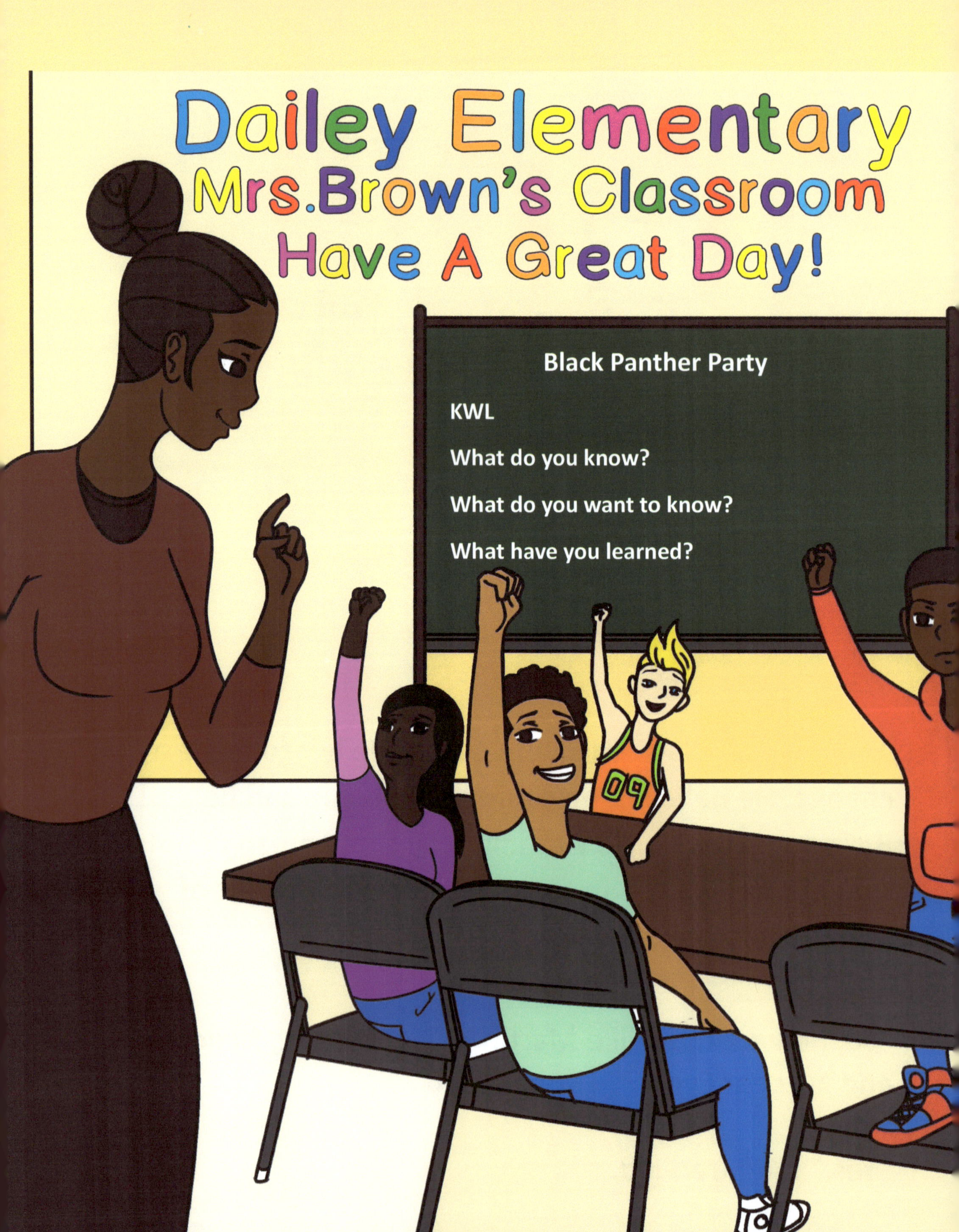
Dailey Elementary
Mrs.Brown's Classroom
Have A Great Day!
Black Panther Party
KWL
What do you know?
What do you want to know?
What have you learned?
09

“I’m so sorry mommy!” Ebony sighed. “Tell me the part about Uncle and me.”

Mom replied, “Alright Ebony. You know that you came from beautiful, smart and strong people. Uncle loved you even though he didn’t meet you. He died so you and I could have a better life. So, children like you could have a better life. I became a teacher to help intelligent children know how incredible they were created and that they could be anything they wanted to be.”

“And, mommy, I do! Thank you, mommy, for buying me clothes and driving me to school.” Ebony gratefully added.

Ebony jumped out of the car, and grabbed her picture of Uncle. She smiled and kissed the picture.

“Thank you, Uncle,” she whispered.

Ebony and Mom walked into the school. Ebony looked up at the beautiful blue sky imagining herself walking with Uncle just as her mom did many, many years ago.

In the hallway, Ebony said to mom,
"When I eat the school breakfast
today, I will remember Uncle. I will
let others know about the Black
Panther Party's free breakfast
program and the 10 rules.
And when I grow up, I will be
like Uncle. I will help my
community just like he did."

"Ubuntu,
Mommy."
Mom walked down
the long hallway
leaving Ebony at the
cafeteria. She heard
Ebony turn and shout,
**"Power to
the People."**

Mom said back, "**All Power to the People**, baby girl."
Then with a big proud smile, mom threw up her fist just the way Uncle would have done.

## Notes to Teachers, Parents, and Students

**This book has true facts about the BPP but is realistic fiction.*

## DID YOU KNOW?

- BPP stands for Black Panther Party.
- BPP was started in 1966 by Huey Newton and Bobby Seale.
- BPP wanted social change.
- BPP was a great help in neighborhoods across the country.

### The Black Panther Party Breakfast for Children Program

The Black Panther Party used a church in Oakland, California to open the first free Breakfast for Children Program in January of 1969. The breakfast program was one of the most effective programs established by the Black Panther Party. It began by feeding a handful of children and spread to tens of thousands of children being fed across the country each day in more than 40 different Black Panther chapters. The mission was to provide a healthy breakfast for school children. The Black Panthers went into the community and requested donations and support. They received it, and the program was a success until it went under attack. That was unfortunate because schools began to see improvements in the academics and behaviors of children participating in the breakfast program.

Mark Clark, leader of the Peoria chapter of the Black Panther Party began a breakfast program in Peoria, IL in the fall of 1969. He solicited the support of a local pastor to feed the children in his city. The children benefited greatly.

The next time you see a picture of a school-age child eating a free breakfast, think about the contributions the BPP made before this became a goal of the USDA.

Brigitte Brown Jackson was born in Peoria, IL but moved to Flint, MI where she spent most of her childhood. She is the maternal niece of slain Black Panther, Mark Clark. Her uncle believed he had to be an activist so she could have a future. His short life provided her a better life. She has used that divine opportunity as a traditional public school teacher and school administrator for several public school academies in Michigan. She has impacted over 2,000 children during her educational career.

She loves calligraphy, writing, and reading. She wants to give children around the world inspiration to creatively read, write and dream big!

She operates the nonprofit, Kingdom Influence, with her husband Willie Jackson. They have eight children and eight grandchildren.

Caleb Price is a writer, illustrator, director, producer, graphic designer, performer and owner of Lighted Righteous. He uses his brilliant imagination to create children books, comics, posters, music, and much more. His Instagram is GreatnessBecomingGreater. Check out his page Lightedrighteous.com.

Michael Martinez is an aspiring Graphic Novelist from Flint, Michigan who wants to make an impact on the people around him. He is a very humble person working towards his dream of becoming the best artist he can be.